for Sebastian with all my love

'de te fabula narratur'

First published 1992 by
Walker Books Ltd, 87 Vauxhall Walk
London SE11 5HJ

© 1992 Debi Gliori

Printed and bound in Hong Kong
by Dai Nippon Printing Co. Ltd

British Library Cataloguing in Publication Data
A catalogue record for this book is available from the British Library.

ISBN 0-7445-2194-7

When I'm BIG

Debi Gliori

WALKER BOOKS
LONDON

When I'm big, I'm going to stay up as late as I like and make myself marshmallows on toast instead of going to bed.

When I'm big, I'm going swimming with the whales in the deep blue sea instead of puddling about in the bath.

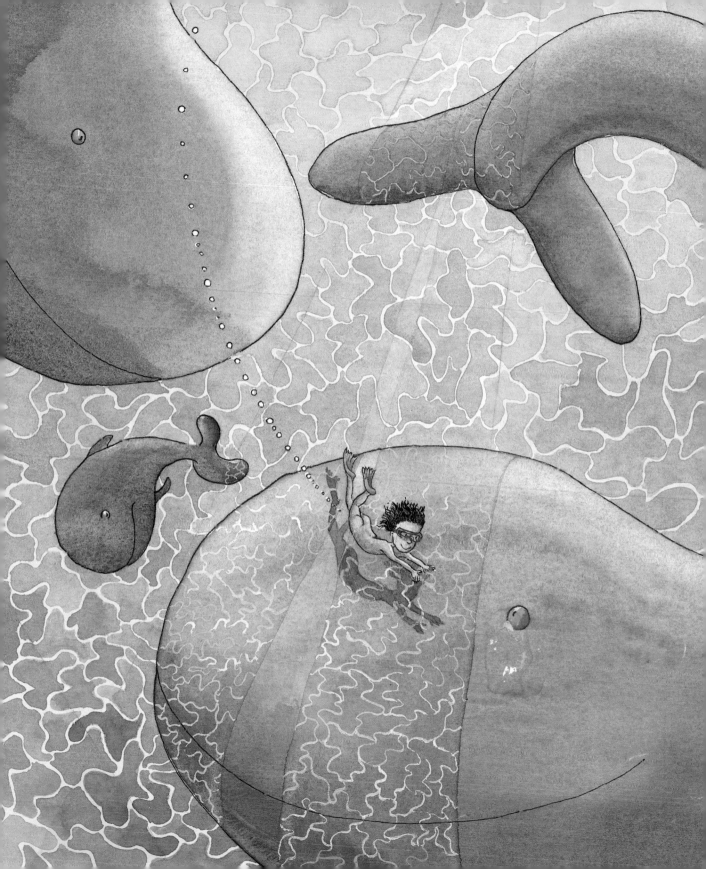

When I'm big,
I'm going to wear
a bird-suit and
gumboots all day
long instead of
a jumper and
dungarees.

When I'm big, I'm going to have a huge back garden with sand mountains that touch the sky and a lake in the middle instead of a sandpit and a paddling pool.

When I'm big, I'm going to drive the trolley round the shops with Dad in it instead of the other way round.

When I'm big, I'm going to grow triffids and Venus fly-traps and man-eating orchids instead of mustard and cress.

When I'm big
I'm going to
ride a proper
bike instead
of a tricycle.

When I'm big, I'm going to have twelve lions, two tigers, a bunch of grizzly bears and a shark instead of a dog, a cat and a goldfish.

When I'm big,
I'm going to put
Mum and Dad
to bed and read
them a story and
turn out the light
and go downstairs
on my own.

I can squeeze
into the safest
place in the world.